For Daisy H

JANETTA OTTER-BARRY BOOKS

TOM TOM THE PIPER'S SON copyright © Frances Lincoln Limited 2011
Text and illustrations copyright © Priscilla Lamont 2011

First published in Great Britain in 2011 and in the USA in 2012 by
Frances Lincoln Children's Books, 4 Torriano Mews,
Torriano Avenue, London NW5 2RZ
www.franceslincoln.com

A catalogue record for this book is available from the British Library
ISBN 978-1-84780-155-5

Illustrated with pen and watercolour
Set in Chalkboard

Printed in Heshan, Guangdong, China by Leo Paper Products Ltd. in May 2011

1 3 5 7 9 8 6 4 2

Nursery Rhyme Crimes

Tom, Tom,
The Piper's Son

by the Pig himself
as told to
PRISCILLA LAMONT

F

FRANCES LINCOLN
CHILDREN'S BOOKS

Tom, Tom, the Piper's son,
Stole a pig and away did run.
The pig was eat and Tom was beat
and Tom went howling down the street.

Tom used to come and play his pipes,
which quite puffed out his cheeks.

No one liked the noise but me,
I loved the squawky squeaks.

I'd dance for him a piggy dance,
or sing a piggy song.

And sometimes, just to make him laugh,
I'd make a piggy pong.

Then one day I heard the words that any pig must dread.

"BACON, HAM and SAUSAGES!"
was what the farmer said.

Next morning Tom soon understood
he mustn't hesitate –

and so we took off on his bike
to save me from my fate.

He pedalled on until at last
we found a lovely wood,

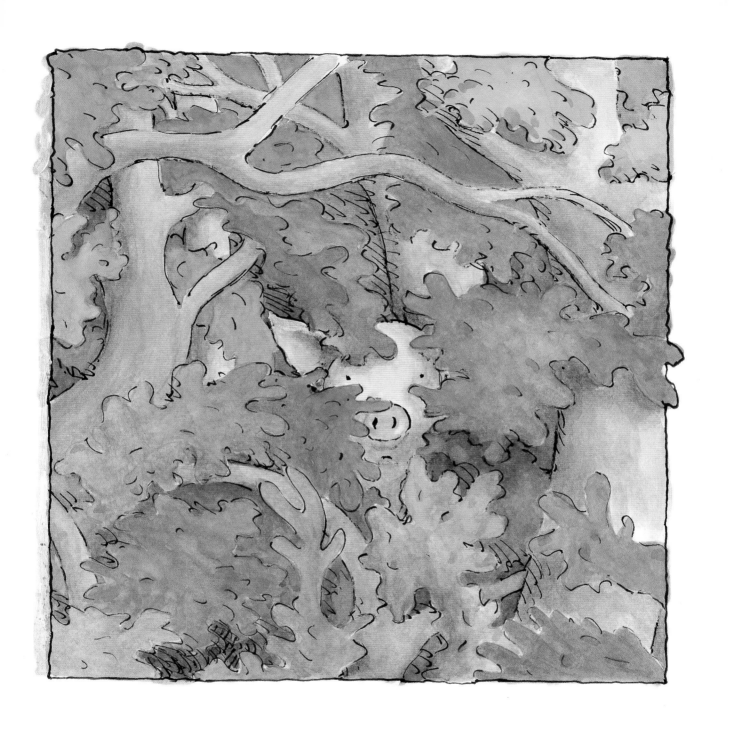

and I hid among the leafy trees
as quickly as I could.

Foxes, squirrels, birds and mice
quite soon came out to play.
They helped me find some food, and then
a nice, warm place to stay.

And now with all my woodland friends
I live without a care.
And if Tom got beat for helping me
it really wasn't fair!

It seems to me a nicer boy
you couldn't hope to meet,
cos thanks to him, as you can see,
I never did get eat!